HOW, HIPPO!

Charles Scribner's Sons New York

"Hang on, Little Hippo!"

Ever since the night he was born in a clump of papyrus stalks at the edge of the cool river, the little hippopotamus stayed close by the side of his mother.

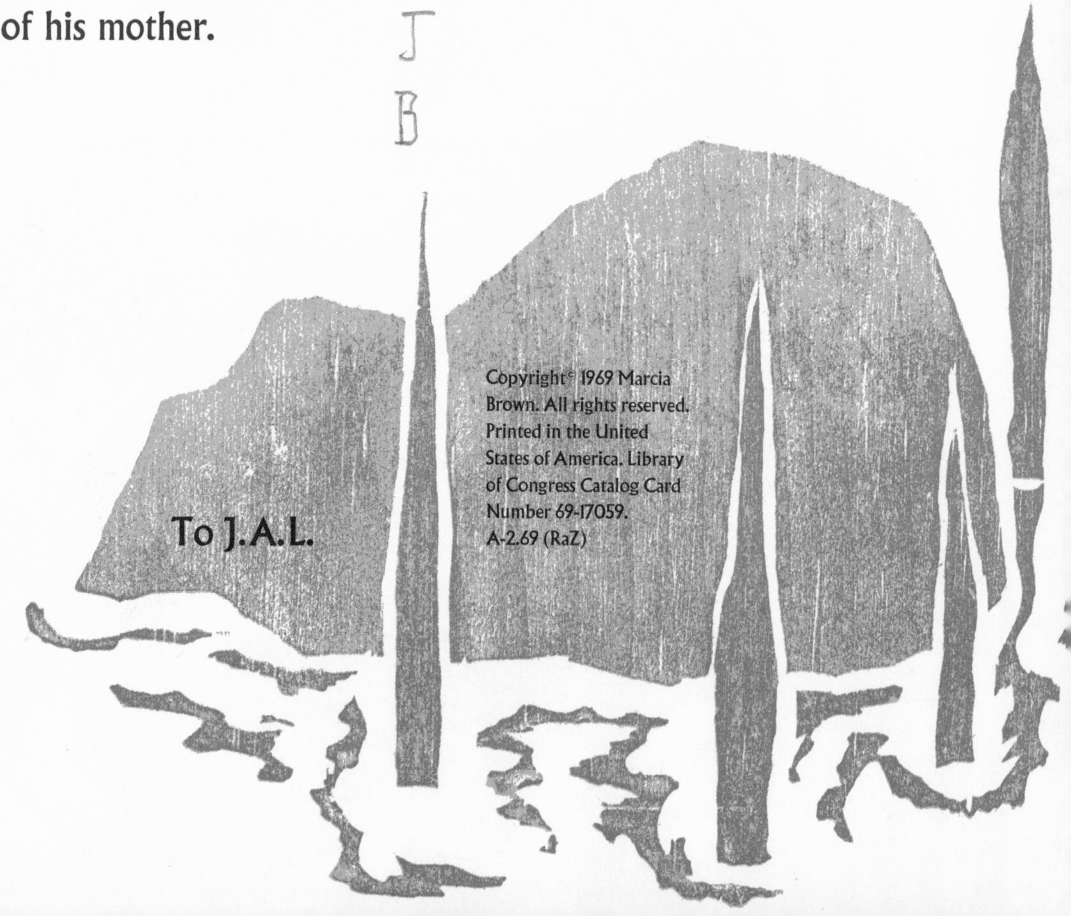

To J.A.L.

Printed in the United States of America. Library of Congress Catalog Card Number 69-17059.
A-2.69 (RaZ)

Snuggled together on the warm sand, or napping in a sunlit pool, the hippos dozed the days away.

When the
cool darkness
fell, Little Hippo
and his mother
made their way up
through the branchy
tunnel from the river
to the feeding ground.
There they ate
the nights away.

The time came for Little Hippo
to learn his grunts and roars.

"How, Hippo!" huffed his mother.

"Huff! Huff! How!"

"How! Hello!"

"How! Watch out!"

"How! Help!"

"Mind your hows, Little Hippo.
Be sure you roar the right one."

Over and over Little Hippo
huffed and snorted his hows.

Little Hippo was never afraid when he was with his mother. Who would bother a huge hippo? But a little hippo . . . ?

"How! Who are you?" he called to the little zebra in the grassy field.

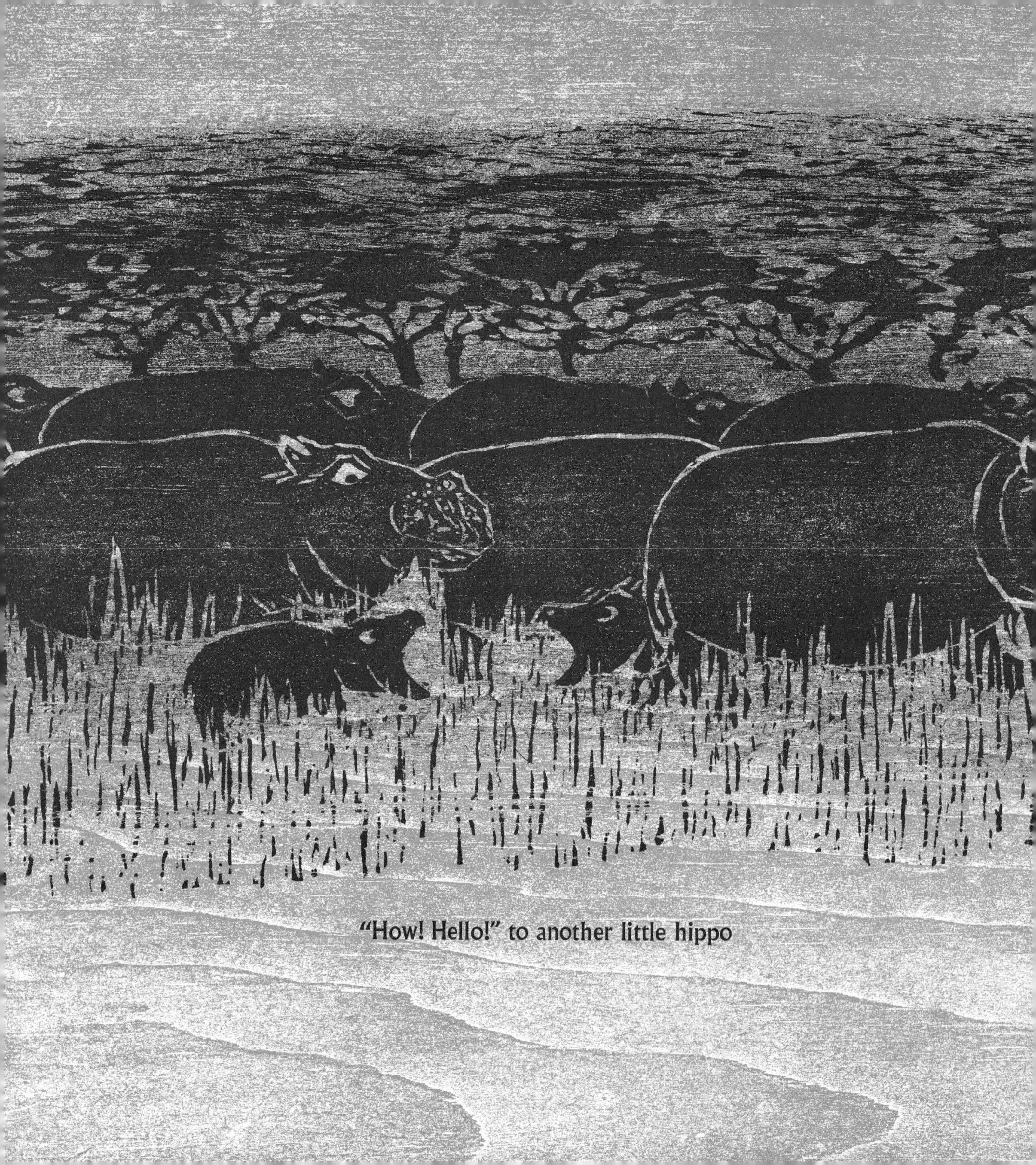

"How! Hello!" to another little hippo

making the long trek for food in the blue night.

“How! Watch out!” to the old buffalo by the water hole, who just looked at him and went on chewing.

One day when the huge hippos were asleep in the warm mud of the still river, Little Hippo bounced up to the surface

to play
with the palm fronds
that dipped
over the water
near the bank.

Silently...

and without a ripple the green-gold eyes glided over the water.

Little Hippo tried to scramble up the bank. But before he could make up his mind

to roar a Help! or a Watch out!
the old crocodile had whipped
around and his great jaws
snapped shut on
Little Hippo's tail.
The crocodile started to drag him
down to the deep water...

"How! HOW!

HOW!"

Mother Hippo heard. She reared up and bellowed.

"How, Hippo! HOW, CROCODILE!"

Scooping up the crocodile in her huge mouth, she waved him in the air and tossed him over her back. When the crocodile opened his mouth to roar with pain

Little Hippo fell free.

That night when Little Hippo and his mother went to the feeding grounds, Mother Hippo warned, "Until you are a huge hippo, remember, a little hippo must mind his hows."

"How, HIPPO!"